For Hester, with great love – G.E.
For Sasha – E.E.

First published in Great Britain in 2013 by
Piccadilly Press, a Templar/Bonnier publishing company
Deepdene Lodge, Deepdene Avenue, Dorking, Surrey RH5 4AT
www.piccadillypress.co.uk

Text copyright © Gareth Edwards, 2013
Illustrations copyright © Elina Ellis, 2013

Designed by Simon Davis
Printed and bound in China by WKT
Colour reproduction by Dot Gradations

ISBN: 978 1 84812 334 2 (h/b)
ISBN: 978 1 84812 333 5 (p/b)

1 3 5 7 9 10 8 6 4 2

THE LITTLEST BIRD

By Gareth Edwards
Illustrated by Elina Ellis

Piccadilly Press

There were seven green birds
in a beautiful nest
at the top of a tree
where the view was the best.

But the Littlest Bird
didn't like it at all
for the beautiful nest
was incredibly small.

No place for her slippers,
her toothbrush and things —
and not even the space
to spread out her wings.

And her brothers and sisters
all borrowed her stuff
and her mum didn't listen
or kiss her enough.

Every night when they tried
to nod off – what a squeeze!
What a wriggling tangle
of feathers and knees!

Every morning
the Littlest Bird really wished
that she didn't wake up
feeling jostled and squished.

So she said to herself,
"I am sick of this place.
They won't care if I move
to a nest with more space."

And she packed up her slippers,
her toothbrush and things
and when no one was looking
she spread out her wings.

Then she fluttered about
over meadow and wood,
looking high, looking low
for a nest that was good.

But the nests that she found
didn't have enough space,
or were gloomy or drafty,
or in the wrong place.

Then on top of a mountain,
she stopped for a rest
and she spotted a simply
INCREDIBLE nest!

It seemed to be empty
with no one in sight,
so she unpacked her things
and moved in for the night.

There was space for her slippers,
her toothbrush and things
and whenever she liked
she could spread out her wings.

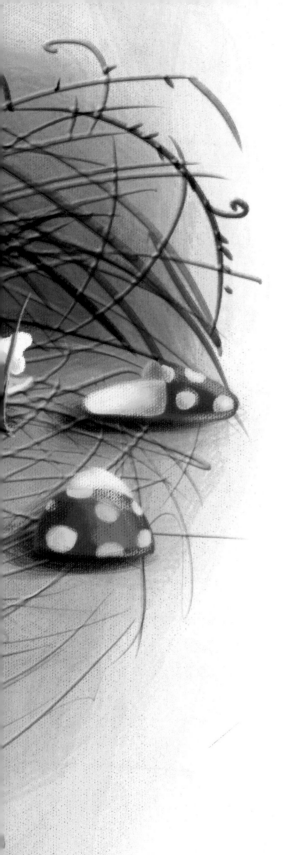

It was strange all the stillness
with no one around . . .

Then the Littlest Bird
heard a loud CRACKING
sound.

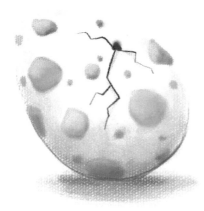

Through a hole
in an egg
poked a
short scaly snout

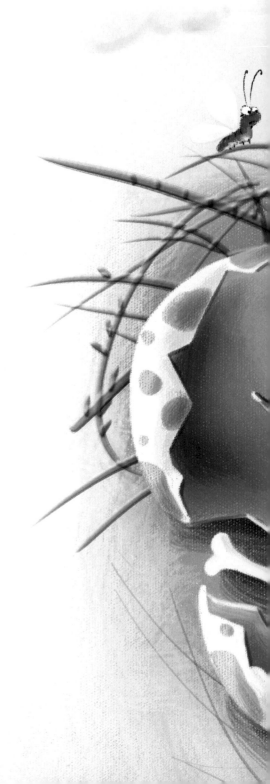

and the beady black eyes
of a dragon peeped out!

"Mummy?" it said
and the Littlest Bird
shook her head at the dragon
but said not a word.

Then she heard a voice calling,
"My baby, I'm here!"
and a big mother dragon
came hurrying near.

The Littlest Bird
watched them cuddle
each other.
She missed her own nest
and she longed
for HER mother.

She looked at the dragons
and felt rather small,
and thought, "Maybe this place
isn't perfect at all."

She packed up her slippers,
her toothbrush and things,
she did not say goodbye,
she just spread out her wings.

Then she took to the air
flying quick as could be
and rushed back to her home
at the top of the tree.

And her mother said, "Darling"
and cuddled and kissed her.
Her brothers and sisters
all said how they'd missed her.

With squishes and squeezes
and flurries of feather
the birds and their mother
all huddled together.

And yes, it was crowded
and ever so small,
but the Littlest Bird
didn't mind that at all!